P9-DFL-073
3 3090 00545 4386

START

To Mom and Baba, who got me hooked on books

A Neal Porter Book
Published by Roaring Brook Press
Roaring Brook Press is a division of Holtzbrinck Publishing Holdings Limited Partnership
175 Fifth Avenue, New York, New York 10010
The art for this book was created with pen and watercolor on paper.
mackids.com

Library of Congress Control Number: 2015951000

ISBN 978-1-62672-333-7

Our books may be purchased in bulk for promotional, educational, or business use. Please contact your local bookseller or the Macmillan Corporate and Premium Sales Department at (800) 221-7945 ext. 5442 or by e-mail at MacmillanSpecialMarkets@macmillan.com.

First edition 2016
Printed in China by Toppan Leefung Printing Ltd., Dongguan City, Guangdong Province
1 3 5 7 9 10 8 6 4 2

FISH

LIAM FRANCIS WALSH

A NEAL PORTER BOOK
ROARING BROOK PRESS
NEW YORK

Q

B
B
FISH

B

FISH

123
816

NI
122
FISH

FINISH
711
401

THE END
410
211
303